DAVID AND GOLIATH

DAVID AND GOLIATH

adapted from the Bible and illustrated by
LEONARD EVERETT FISHER

Holiday House/New York

E

G

Copyright © 1993 by Leonard Everett Fisher
ALL RIGHTS RESERVED
Printed in the United States of America
FIRST EDITION

Library of Congress Cataloging-in-Publication Data
Fisher, Leonard Everett.
David & Goliath / adapted from the Bible and illustrated by
Leonard Everett Fisher.—1st ed.
p.   cm.
Summary: Retells the Bible story in which a Hebrew shepherd boy
kills the giant Philistine warrior Goliath with a slingshot.
ISBN 0-8234-0997-X
1. David, King of Israel—Juvenile literature.   2. Goliath
(Biblical giant)—-Juvenile literature.   3. Bible stories—O.T.
[1. David, King of Israel.   2. Goliath (Biblical giant)   3. Bible
stories—O.T.]   I. Title.   II. Title: David and Goliath.
BS580.D3F577   1993   92-24063   CIP   AC
222′.4309505—dc20

Nile River

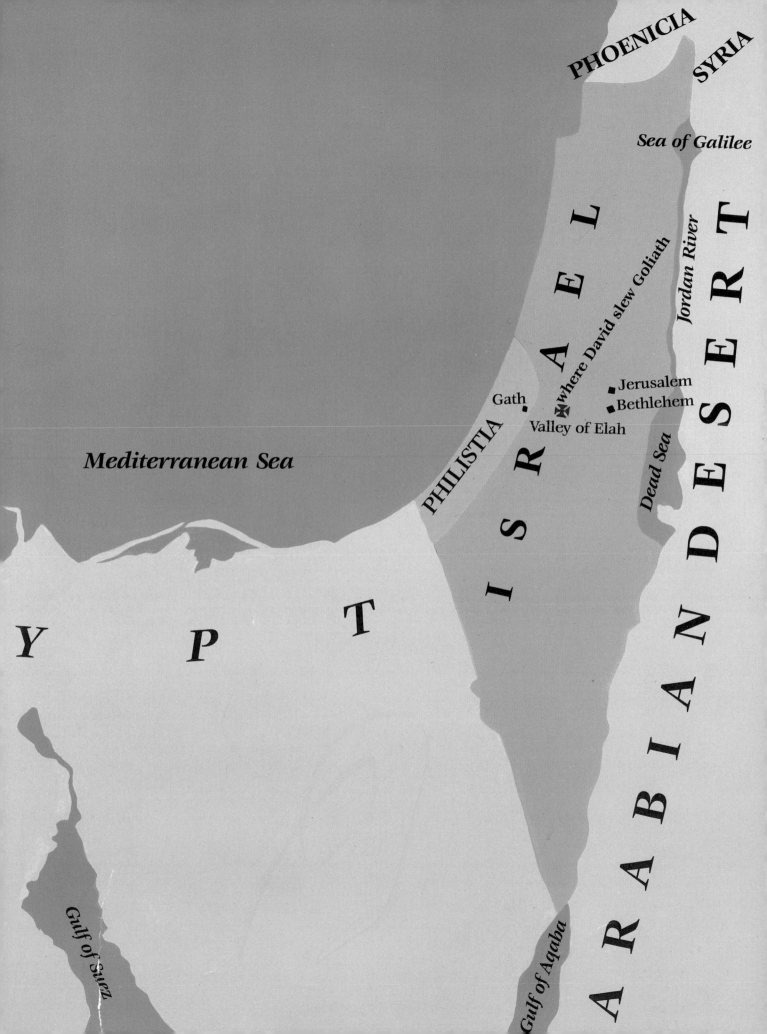

David, son of Jesse the Israelite, played his harp while he tended his flock of sheep on the grassy hills of Bethlehem. The music of David's harp filled all who heard it with joy.

One day Jesse told David, "Messengers have come from King Saul. They say that the king is filled with dark spirits. He wants you to come to the palace in Jerusalem and play for him there."

David went to Jerusalem and strummed his harp for the king. Saul smiled when he heard the sweet music. As the dark spirits vanished, he said, "I need you to stay so I can listen to the sound of your harp." And David obeyed him.

Soon after, Saul heard that his enemies, the Philistines, were marching toward Jerusalem. He gathered the men of Israel around him. Among them were David's brothers. They formed an army and went forth to meet the enemy.

David was too young to fight. King Saul sent him back to Bethlehem to tend his sheep. The soft melodies of David's harp could once again be heard throughout the hills of Bethlehem.

But David was restless. "Why can't I fight like my brothers?" he asked his father. "Didn't I once kill a lion and a bear when they stole our sheep?"

"You are not old enough to be a soldier," said Jesse. "But you can take this cheese, bread, and corn to your brothers on the battlefield."

David rose early the next morning and set out to find his brothers.

As the sun burned red hot in the sky, David reached the valley of Elah. There, he saw two mighty armies prepared for battle. The Philistines stood on the mountain slope on one side of the valley; the Israelites faced them from the other side.

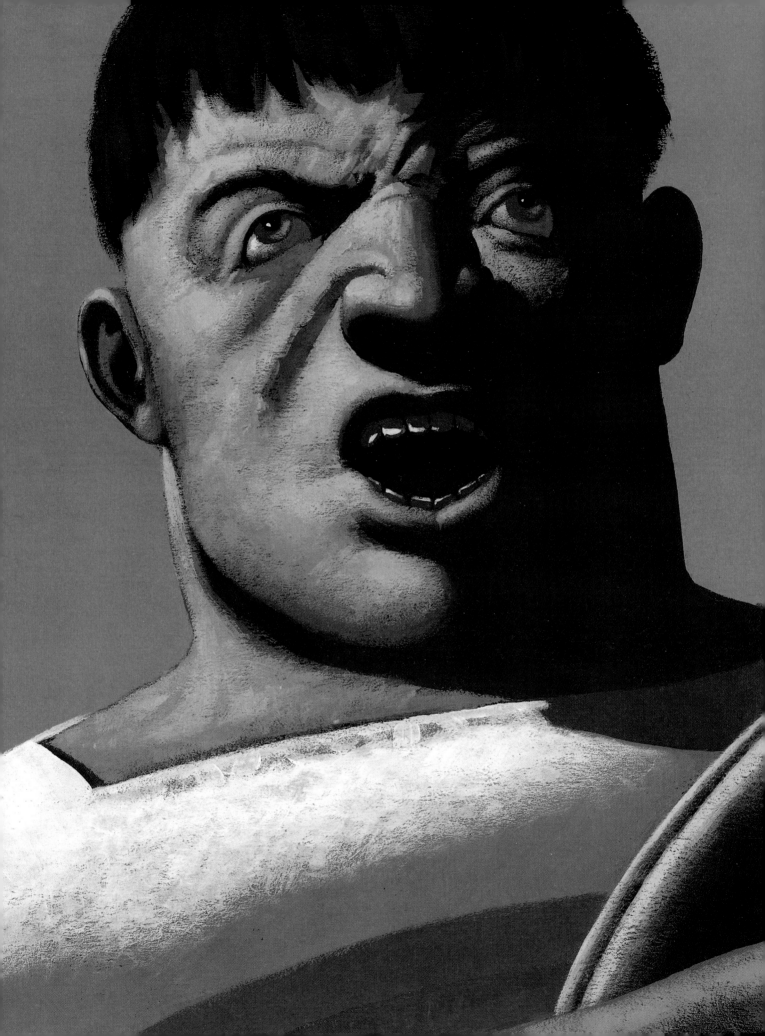

Suddenly, a giant warrior strode out of the Philistine camp. He was ten feet tall and as solid as a granite block. His sword and shield glittered in the bright sun.

"Hear me, Israelites! I am Goliath of Gath," he roared, his deep voice rumbling like thunder up and down the valley. "Choose a man among you to fight me. If he wins, we are your slaves. If he loses, you are ours!"

King Saul and his soldiers trembled when they heard Goliath's words. No one was big enough or strong enough to battle the giant and win.

"Why have your hearts failed you?" David asked. "Is there not one of you to stand up to this Philistine?"

No one spoke. Not even the king.

"If none of you is brave enough to fight the giant, then I shall," said David.

"Go home, David," replied King Saul, "and mind your sheep. You are just a shepherd boy. Goliath is a warrior. He is twice as big as you."

"God gave me the strength to slay a lion and a bear that stole our sheep," said David. "He shall give me the strength to slay Goliath, too, and you shall have his head."

"Then go," said King Saul. "May God watch over you."

Saul offered David armor for protection, but David refused to wear it. The armor was too heavy. Instead, he picked up five stones and put them in a sack. Then, with nothing more than the stones and a sling, David went down to meet Goliath in the valley of Elah.

When Goliath saw David he burst out laughing. "Isra-elites! You insult me," he bellowed. "You have sent a boy to fight a man. His flesh and bones will feed birds and beasts."

"I come to you in the name of God," David called out to the giant. "It will be your flesh and bones that will feed birds and beasts, not mine."

Goliath shook his sword. David quickly placed a stone in his sling and flung it at the giant. The stone whistled across the valley and struck Goliath in the forehead. The giant fell.

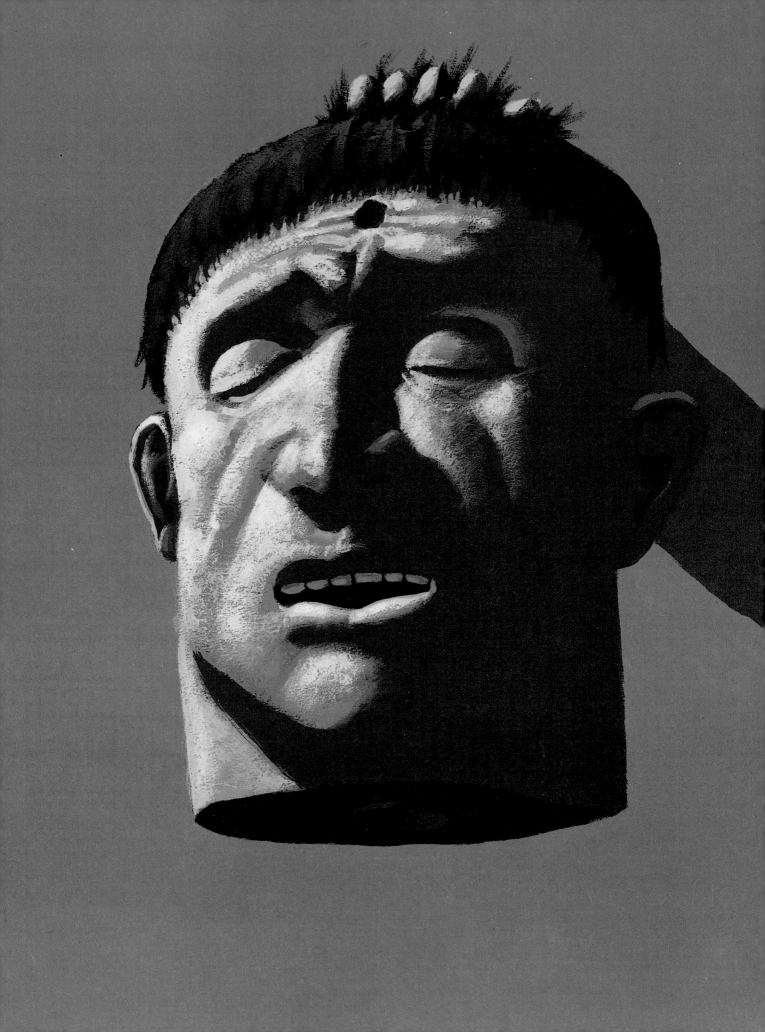

David approached Goliath's body. He took the giant's sword, and with one swift stroke, cut off his head.

"Here is Goliath, our enemy," cried David as he raised the head high in victory.

The Philistines turned and fled.

David, the shepherd boy, had saved the land of the Israelites.

One day he would be their king.